Scholastic's
# The Magic School Bus®
## MEETS THE ROT SQUAD
### A Book About Decomposition
TM

Scholastic Inc.
New York   Toronto   London   Auckland   Sydney

Based on the episode of the animated TV series,
written by John May and Jocelyn Stevenson.
Produced by Scholastic Productions, Inc.
Based on *The Magic School Bus* books
written by Joanna Cole and illustrated by Bruce Degen.

*TV tie-in book adaptation by Linda Beech*
*and illustrated by Carolyn Bracken*
*TV script written by John May and Jocelyn Stevenson*

ISBN 0-590-40023-1

12 11 10 9 8 7 6 5 4       7 8 9/9 0/0

Printed in the U.S.A.      23

First Scholastic printing, October 1995

"Ah, the smell of a rotting orange!" Ms. Frizzle was thrilled. Our class was having a disgusting, gross rot contest, and Ralphie's orange was really rotten. The judges gave him two nose holds and a faint.

Science is a little different in Ms. Frizzle's class.

Then it was Wanda's turn. She had something really rotten in a plastic tub. It looked all black and moldy. "It's been in my refrigerator since I was four years old," she told us.

The Friz could hardly wait to see what it was. Whatever it was, the judges gave Wanda three faints. She was the winner.

"To congratulate you," said Ms. Frizzle, "I have a little prize." Then she gave Wanda a baby tree.

Wanda seemed confused. "I really like it," she said, "but it's not rotten or anything, is it?"

Keesha said, "It's so . . . alive."

"That's right, Keesha," said the Friz. "It's very alive, and so is rot!"

Really? We were very surprised.

Wanda said she wanted to plant her tree in an empty lot near her home.

"To the bus, class. Two by two," said Ms. Frizzle. And in no time we were riding through town.

On the way Keesha asked, "Why do you want to put your nice tree in that ugly old lot?"

"It's filled with lots of dead stuff," added Carlos.

"That's the point," said Wanda. "We can make the lot beautiful. We'll clear out all the dead stuff and plant my lovely tree."

"The tree will look great when it gets big," Wanda told us. "The lot can become a little park. We could call it Wanda World!"

"What about a theme park?" Carlos suggested.

"And the theme could be rot!" cried Dorothy Ann. "We'll call it Rot Land."

Keesha wanted to open a restaurant. Phoebe wanted to build a recycling center.

Wanda had other plans.

We could serve rot dogs!

What a rotten joke!

The bus stopped at the lot. "Ms. Frizzle, I'm going to go out and have a look," Wanda said.

Ms. Frizzle nodded. "Take chances," she called after Wanda. "Get messy. Make mistakes!"

While we were still thinking of ways to use the lot, Wanda saw a sign:

Without telling anyone, Wanda ran to a phone booth and called Larry. He promised to come and clean up the lot right away.

When Wanda returned to the bus, we were still arguing about what to do.

Then Arnold shouted, "Hold it! Why not leave this place just the way it is? If you leave nature alone, it'll get along just fine."

Wanda didn't agree. "That rotten log has got to go. It's dead! It's useless," she said. "I mean, look at it."

That was all Ms. Frizzle needed to hear. "Seat belts, everyone!" called the Friz. The bus began to shake and shrink with us in it. The next thing we knew, we were smaller, and driving over a log in the lot.

"We're going to find out what rot has to do with life," the Friz explained.

Wanda didn't seem to be enjoying our field trip. "We've got to go!" she kept yelling.

The rest of us were busy dodging beetles, termites, and a chipmunk. They seemed so big because we were so little.

At my old school, we were bigger than the bugs.

Then Ralphie pointed to a hole.

"Our rotten field trip has just begun," said the Friz. And she marched us down the hole into the log. We entered a dark tunnel.

Suddenly, we heard a strange sound. It was a wood-pecker looking for its dinner.

"Don't worry," said Ms. Frizzle. "Woodpeckers only eat bugs."

The problem was, we were the same size as bugs.

Something big and scary came toward us from the other end of the tunnel. Ms. Frizzle said it was a bessie bug — a kind of beetle.

"They make the tunnels in the log," she explained.

We were glad when the bus squeezed its way through the tunnel. It looked a little different, though. We followed the bus down the tunnel.

We came to a place with lots of threads. Dorothy Ann told us they were from mushrooms that grew on the outside of the log. "According to my research, they eat the wood and help rot the log," she said.

"Who would have known a dead log could be so full of life?" said Keesha.

Wanda was still trying to get us out of there. "We might become somebody's lunch," she warned.

This didn't bother the Friz. She jumped on a slimy slide and yelled for us to follow.

"It's a slime mold — a kind of fungus," she said. "Another living thing living off the log."

Ms. Frizzle pointed out a family of mice sleeping in the log. "See? The log gives some animals shelter," she said.

"You know," said Dorothy Ann, "this place is stunningly stupendous just the way it is."

"Wait!" said Wanda. "What about taking this log away?"

"Sorry, Wanda. We've changed our minds," Carlos told her.

"Hey, welcome to the Keep the Log as It Is Club," said Arnold. He gave Dorothy Ann and Carlos special badges.

At my old school, we had sandwiches for lunch.

Lunchtime!

Just then the Friz called, "Lunchtime, class!"
We were all very hungry, but the menu bugged us.
"Log nuggets? Wood dumplings? Bark pudding?"
asked Ms. Frizzle.
When Ralphie asked for real food, she said, "The
log *is* food. That's the beauty of it."
She pointed to all the living things that used the
log for food and energy.

"So let's just get out of here and open our own restaurant," said Wanda. As she spoke, a beetle ran by and caught a grub.

"The beetle is having the grub for lunch," said Ralphie.

"Right," agreed Keesha. "Everywhere you look, it's lunchtime."

Ralphie nodded. "This place is *already* a restaurant. Sorry, Wanda, we don't want to clear it away anymore."

"Two more for the Keep the Log as It Is Club," yelled Arnold. He passed out badges to Keesha and Ralphie.

We came to a really mushy part of the log. "Decomposition. Isn't it wonderful?" sighed the Friz. "It breaks everything down into smaller pieces." She pointed out some rotten examples.

"Okay," agreed Wanda, "but these creatures leave a lot of litter, don't they? You know, bug plops!"

"The bug plops are being eaten by other bugs, too," Phoebe told her.

"It's natural recycling," added Tim.

Wanda thought it was gross, but Ms. Frizzle said it was all part of decomposition.

"Oh, I give up," said Wanda. *"Now let's just get out of here!"*

But Keesha was calling to us from the very end of the rotten log. She had found something else. "Look! Beautiful, rich soil!" she exclaimed.

"It's perfect for your tree, Wanda," said Arnold as we raced down to meet her. Arnold and Keesha started to sing.

An old dead log sitting on your lawn;
It's ugly, it's awful, and you want it gone.

Well, that log you've got is not a blot
Cause it's got rot . . . and that's a lot.

It's breaking down . . . are you wondering how?
Well, fungus and bugs — they use it for chow.

It's rained on by rain, snowed on by snow,

Breaks down into soil,
so new things can grow.

It's cool, it's renewal — just ask Ms. Frizzle.
That log's just fine the way it izzle.

Wanda finally understood. "This place is fine, just the way it is. There is no reason to take this log away," she told us.

But just then a car door slammed.

Wanda gulped. "No reason . . . except one," she said.

"What's that?" asked Carlos.

"Larry," Wanda gulped as a giant boot came down near where we stood. The ground shook, and so did we.

We began to run.

"This way, class!" Ms. Frizzle called, and we dashed under the log. Outside, we could hear the sound of a chain saw.

"Is there something you'd like to tell us?" the Friz asked Wanda.

Then we found out about Wanda's call to Larry. We could tell she felt bad. We all did.

Rat-a-tat-tat!

Poor log!

Poor us!

While we were shaking and quaking, Wanda thought of a plan. She explained it to Ms. Frizzle.

"Good idea," said the Friz. Then she whistled to the bus.

"Come on, guys. I need your help," said Wanda, and we all began to dig out the bus.

Then Wanda opened a hatch on the bus. She tossed us all funny-looking costumes. "Put these on and hurry! We're going to be log gremlins."

"You have got to be joking," said Ralphie.

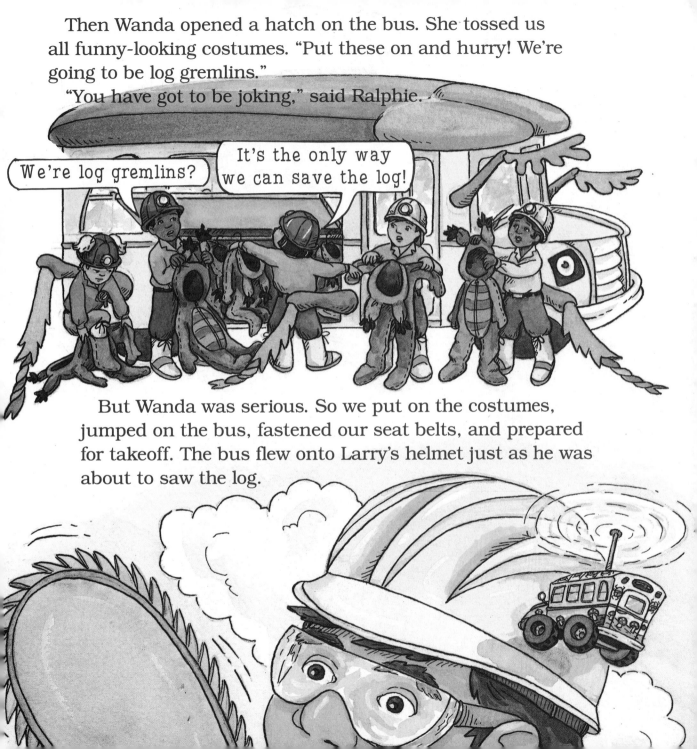

We're log gremlins?

It's the only way we can save the log!

But Wanda was serious. So we put on the costumes, jumped on the bus, fastened our seat belts, and prepared for takeoff. The bus flew onto Larry's helmet just as he was about to saw the log.

Then we all climbed out, and Wanda started shouting to Larry. He was certainly surprised. Log gremlins were new to him.

"What do you see when you look around here?" Wanda asked him.

"A routine log removal," answered Larry.

"Well, look again," said Wanda. Then she told Larry about all the life in the log. She explained that rot is wonderful and necessary.

"All those creatures are nature's Rot Squad. They're how nature recycles itself and makes new from the old," she said.

Larry looked . . .

and listened . . .

and then he left.

So did we.

"Log gremlins," we heard him mutter. "How come I've never heard of them before?"

"That gremlin idea was a stroke of genius," said Arnold.

"Thanks, Arn," said Wanda. "But from now on I'm going to leave rot alone."

Back in the classroom, there was another surprise — the bucket of rot from our contest. It was so smelly it was hard to ignore!

"Everybody back on the bus!" shouted Wanda. "I've got another rotten idea!"

We couldn't believe it.

"Rot is an important part of nature," she said. "It provides food for other living things. So this rot will be a treat for my tree!"

Ms. Frizzle said, "As I always say, it doesn't have to be delicious to be nutritious."

We all laughed. Then Wanda recycled our rot right in that lot.

That's a *lot* of *rot!*

# A Few More Rotten Thoughts

*Rrrrring.*

**Producer:** Hello. This is the Magic School Bus.

**Caller:** That show was rotten.

**Producer:** Thank you.

**Caller:** But not all rotten things are filled with bugs.

**Producer:** Right. Lots of rot is caused by things that are too small to see — like bacteria.

**Caller:** So? Why weren't bacteria in the show?

**Producer:** We wanted to shrink down to the size of bacteria, but Arnold wouldn't go.

**Caller:** Is there anything that doesn't rot?

**Producer:** Not if it was once alive. Plants, animals, bacteria — all decompose after they die.

**Caller:** A log fell near my house. When's it going to rot?

**Producer:** It has already started, but rot can take a long time — years, even.

**Caller:** Another thing — you left out one of my favorite creatures, the earthworm.

**Producer:** Whoops!

**Caller:** Earthworms are very good at eating and plowing and improving the soil.

**Producer:** Then that's what they should be left to do.

**Caller:** What if there were no rot? What if nothing ever decayed?

**Producer:** The soil wouldn't get back the nutrients or food that plants need to grow. So the plants would die.

**Caller:** One more thing. Are there really log gremlins?

**Producer:** Well, er . . . Larry thought so.

**Caller:** Hmmm . . .

16441

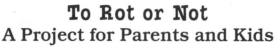

# To Rot or Not
## A Project for Parents and Kids

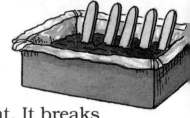

Ms. Frizzle's class learned that rot is important. It breaks things up, and it helps the soil. So what about things that don't rot? What happens to them? Try this to find out.

1. Line the inside of a shoebox with plastic.

2. Fill the shoebox halfway with soil from outside.

3. Bury five things — some grapes, a safety pin, a piece of paper, a lettuce leaf, a ballpoint pen — a few inches deep in the box.

4. Label five Popsicle sticks with the names of the things you buried. Place these in the soil as markers.

5. Make a chart like the one below. Tell what you think will happen. After several weeks, check to see what does happen.

| Garbage | My Prediction | My Observation |
|---|---|---|
| grapes | | |
| safety pin | | |
| paper | | |
| lettuce leaf | | |
| ballpoint pen | | |

**Something to Think About:** What happens to things that rot when you throw them away? What happens to things that don't rot? Why is it important to recycle things that rot?